All You Need
for a Beach

To Jen and Drew, Spence and Dylan, Kate and John
—A. S.

For Justus . . . I know those toes
—B. L.

All You Need for a Beach

Alice Schertle

ILLUSTRATED BY

Barbara Lavallee

SILVER WHISTLE/HARCOURT, INC.

Orlando   Austin   New York   San Diego   Toronto   London

Printed in Singapore

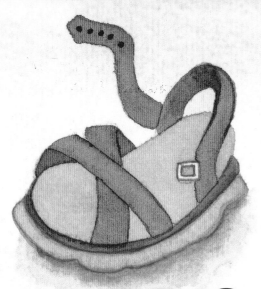

One grain of sand
like the smallest seed,

one
tiny
grain,

that's all you need
for a beach!

EXCEPT FOR

five million other grains,
ten million more,

spread them all out
on a sandy shore....

Trillions of grains of sand,

   and EACH

is one small piece
of your very own beach!
   Great!

WAIT!

One thing more
before
you're done:

Don't forget to add the sun.
(You'll just need one.)

BUT

now you've got
a beach that's *hot*!

You'll need

a yellow umbrella,
a circle of shade,
sunglasses,
beach towel,
lemonade,

bucket and
shovel,
big blue ball,

and that's *all*.

EXCEPT FOR

the seagulls.
Plenty of those.
Some in the sky,
some making rows
of seagull tracks
where the sand is wet—

WET?

Wet, you say?
How did the sand get
wet that way?

A beach needs sand
that's wet and squishy,
waves rolling in
all foamy and fishy.

A beach needs an *ocean*
sparkly blue—

better add that, too.

NOW

you're through.

Sand and sea,
sun and shade,
buckets and balls and
lemonade,
fish in the water,
birds on the wing . . .
You really don't need another thing.

EXCEPT FOR

a couple of sails,
three or four whales,
pelicans fishing—

LOOK OUT!

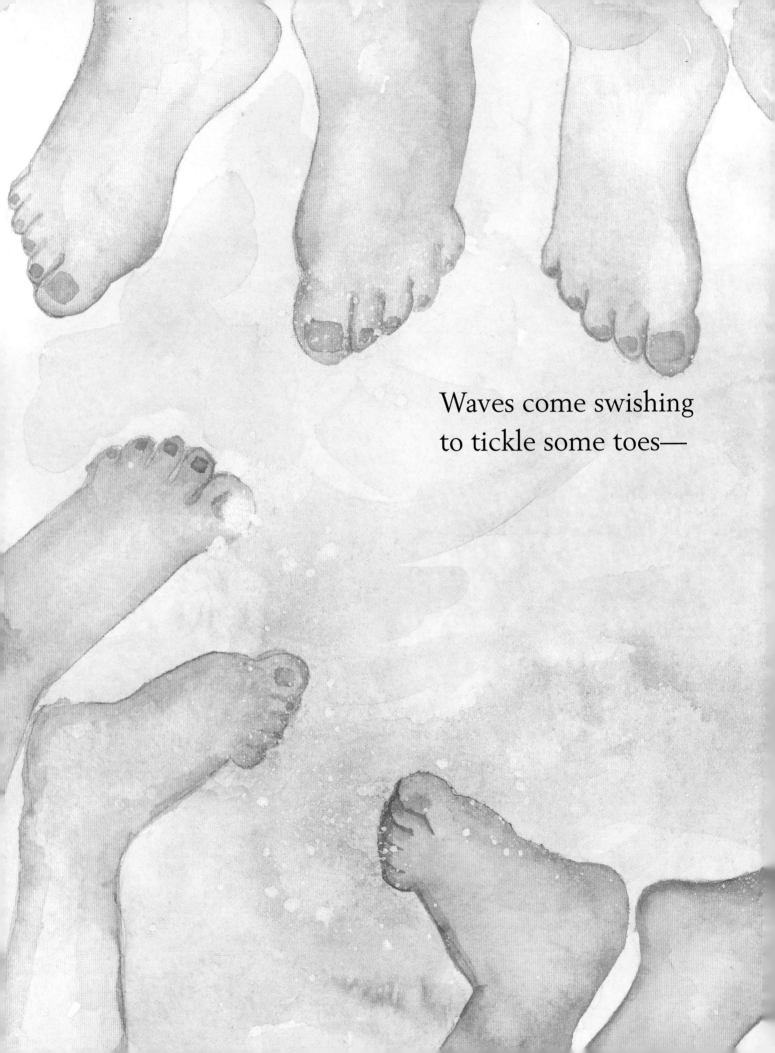

Waves come swishing
to tickle some toes—

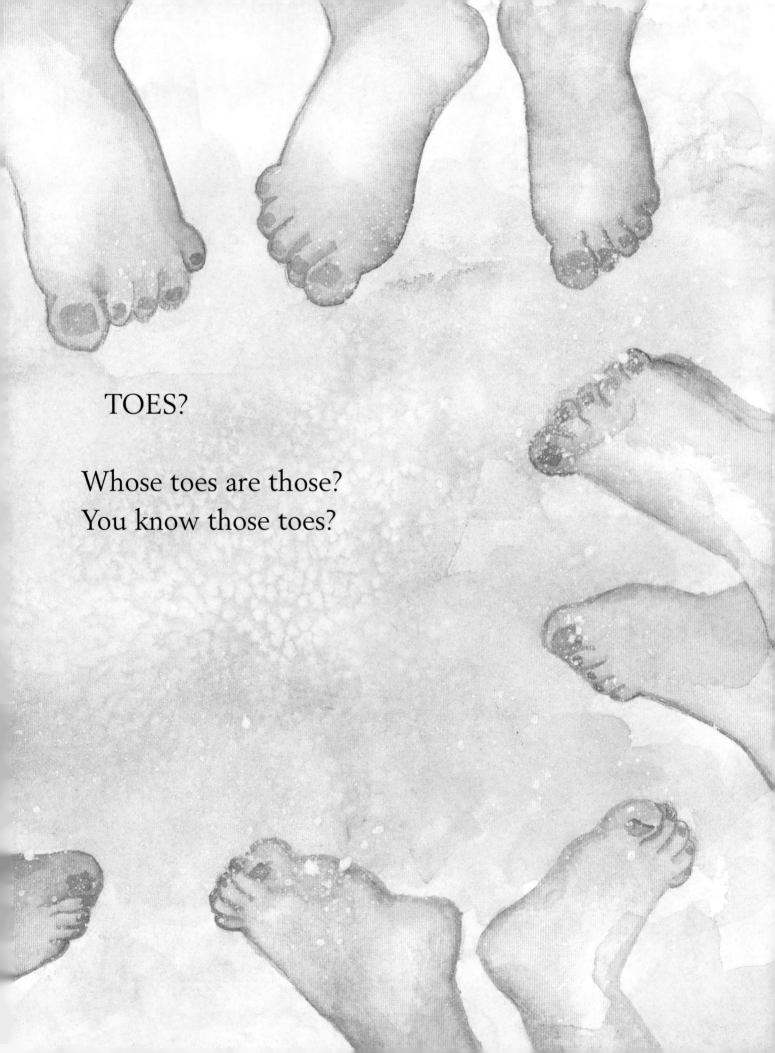

TOES?

Whose toes are those?
You know those toes?

Ten toes belonging
to you-know-who.

All you need for a beach is . . .

YOU!

Library of Congress Cataloging-in-Publication Data
Schertle, Alice.
All you need for a beach/Alice Schertle; illustrated by Barbara Lavallee.
p. cm.
"Silver Whistle."
Summary: Rhyming text describes all of the items essential for fun at the beach,
from the first grain of sand to the bucket and shovel and the ten toes tickled by a wave.
[1. Beaches—Fiction. 2. Stories in rhyme.] I. Lavallee, Barbara, ill. II. Title.
PZ8.3.S29717Al 2004
[E]—dc21   2002151775
ISBN 0-15-216755-2

First edition
A   C   E   G   H   F   D   B
Printed in Singapore

The illustrations in this book were done in watercolor and gouache on watercolor paper.
The display type and text type were set in Berling.
Color separations by Bright Arts Ltd., Hong Kong
Printed and bound by Tien Wah Press, Singapore
This book was printed on totally chlorine-free Stora Enso Matte paper.
Production supervision by Sandra Grebenar and Ginger Boyer
Designed by Linda Lockowitz